THE MISSING CORPSE

(THE LAKESIDE COZY CAT MYSTERIES SERIES)

Janet Evans

CHAPTER 1

Meoooow!

Susan Becker turned around quickly at the sound of breaking glass and her best friend's indignant cry. "Mr. Giles," she called out to the large gray cat who was both her best friend and, at times, a nuisance. Times like now, to be precise. The cat continued across the kitchen counter until he reached the end, and then he gracefully leapt across the aisle and landed on the center island.

She looked at what used to be a very nice glass mixing bowl, now lying on the linoleum in pieces, as the flour that had been inside it slowly floated to the floor. "Look at the mess."

She shook her head and walked around the counter to check on her cat. Mr. Giles seemed unperturbed by the mess he'd caused. He sat on the opposite side of the bakery kitchen, blinking his light green eyes at her. Something metallic glinted at his feet. Before she could get close enough to see exactly what treasure he'd brought her this time, two things happened - the oven timer went off, and the buzzer above the bakery's front door rang out.

"Guess this will have to wait a few minutes." She looked at the cat and then pointed a finger in his direction. "Don't get into any more trouble."

She turned off the kitchen timer, grabbed the hot pads, and then carefully pulled the trays of cupcakes from the oven to set them on the cooling racks. When all eight pans were cooling nicely, she tossed the hot pads to the counter and went out to greet her first customer of the day.

Glancing at the clock just above the kitchen door, she was amazed to see that it was already seven on what she hoped was a beautiful Wednesday morning. Since she started her workday somewhere around 3:30, she never knew what was happening outside until she came to the front of the bakery to turn the open sign around. It could be raining, or a beautiful sunshiny day, but in the back of the kitchen it was always the same.

She'd purchased the small bakery with a small business loan right after graduating from college and currently lived in the two bedroom apartment located directly above the retail space. Her shop was situated on the main street running through Lakeside, a small resort town of a few thousand people located at the far edge of Lake Taneycomo. Its location near Branson meant it had a steady stream of tourists coming through during the summer, providing the locals with a source of income that helped them weather the winter months.

It was currently mid-July, and this tourist season had been one of the best since Susan had opened up her small bakery. She used her hands to make sure her hair hadn't escaped the confines of her hairnet and then plastered a smile on her face. *Time to greet the customers.*

When she pushed through the swinging door, her smile grew bigger. "Detective Fletcher, I don't usually see you out and about quite this early."

Detective Kip Fletcher was in charge of all missing persons and homicides in the small town of Lakeside-- a job he'd once hoped would be quiet enough to give him time to pursue several cold case financial crimes going back to the Silverado era of the late eighties and early nineties. It was like hunting for treasure, he'd once told Susan. Sometimes you recovered enough money to earn a handsome cash reward.

 Of course, Susan was hunting for something else. But she wouldn't let herself think about that right now.

 Anyway, in the last ten months, Kip had been too busy to work his cold cases. There had already been three murders in their fair town, more than the entire decade before that. Fletcher had solved all three cases-- but he'd had a little bit of help from Susan and her cat. Of course she'd graciously allowed him to take full credit.

"Good morning, Suzie. I thought I saw Mr. Giles sneaking around the side of the building a few minutes ago."

"He just came in through the back window. I installed that pet door down low for him, but will he use it? No. He continues to insist on entering through the window."

"Maybe cats are a lot like dogs?" Kip took a large bite out of the cinnamon roll she handed him while closing his eyes to savor the cinnamon, sugar, and pecans. Delicious.

"Mr. Giles is definitely not up for learning any new tricks," Susan said. "That cat is more set in his ways than I am."

Kip smiled at her and then lowered his voice as another patron entered the bakery. "Well, I like your ways just fine." When her face flushed bright red, he chuckled.

Trying to regain her composure, Susan fanned her face with a hand. "Did you come in here to give me a hard time, or did you want something?"

"I came in here for a box of doughnuts to take into work and to tell you that we had another crime committed last night."

Susan grabbed an empty box and began filling it with a variety of doughnuts. "What kind of crime?"

"Grave robbing," Kip said.

Susan paused. "Grave robbing?" When Kip nodded, she put the last doughnut in the box and secured the lid. "So, you're saying someone dug up a grave last night?"

"Yes, ma'am. That's what I'm saying." Kip took the box of doughnuts from her hand and handed over the appropriate cash.

"Well, are they going to re-bury the casket? Whose grave did they dig up?" A bunch more questions were racing through her head, but she was prevented from asking them by his next statement.

Kip lowered his voice. "They can't re-bury the casket."

"How come?" Susan asked, thinking it would be simple enough since the hole was already dug. Just push the casket back into the hole and cover it up with dirt. Ten minutes with a backhoe. Simple. Easy. Problem solved.

"Think you've got it all figured out, don't you? Well, you might want to consider one more piece of evidence." Kip still wasn't sure how he felt about her amateur detective work. She'd been instrumental in helping solve several tough cases in the last year, but each time she'd placed herself in serious danger. He definitely didn't like that.

Susan grinned at him, loving the little game they often played where he kept back some of the facts. She crossed her arms over her chest. "What haven't you told me?" Kip knew she loved a good mystery. Judging from the look in his eyes, he knew she was going to find his next words irresistible.

Kip lowered his voice to barely a whisper. "They took the corpse, but left the casket."

CHAPTER 2

They took the corpse but left the casket? Eewww!

"Someone stole a dead body?" she asked in a voice barely above a whisper. She glanced at her waiting customers, pleased to see that they were consumed with whatever bit of news was filtering into their smartphones. Their eyes seemed glued to the cellular devices in their hands, and they didn't seem in the least perturbed that she wasn't helping them yet.

Kip nodded. "Yeah." Another set of customers entered the bakery. "Looks like it's time for me to go. How about lunch?"

It was the town busybody, Mrs. Carruthers, and her group of cronies. All three women had been married to influential men once upon a time. Now that they were widowed with all of their children grown up and moved away, they had taken it upon themselves to snoop into everyone's business. Even the tourists weren't immune to their meddling ways.

Susan shook her head. "Julie doesn't work today. How about dinner?" Julie Hanson was a local high school student who helped out in the bakery some afternoons. On Wednesdays she had the day off to participate in the high school marching band. Susan glanced at Mrs. Carruthers, seeing the calculating gleam in the woman's eyes when she saw her talking to Kip. Their conversation needed to end. Now.

"You cooking?" he asked with a hopeful look in his eyes.

"Sure," she said. "You bring the meat, and I'll supply everything else. Have a nice day." She headed towards her next customers, smiling at the three older women as she passed them. "I'll be with you ladies in just a minute."

The tourists were still deciding which of her morning treats they were going to indulge in, giving her another few seconds to look towards the front door. Kip was already across the street and climbing into his patrol vehicle.

"I think we're ready to order," the younger of the two tourists told her.

"Great! What did you decide on?"

"Those cinnamon rolls look absolutely divine, but I truly don't want to know how many calories are in them."

Susan grinned at her. "How about you enjoy your vacation and forget about calories for a day?"

The woman looked thoughtful and then nodded her head eagerly. "In that case, give me two of them. If I'm going to blow it, I'm going to do it in style."

Her friend ordered the same thing, and then they both ordered up large coffees as well. Susan bid them a good day and turned to wait on the older women. "Good morning, ladies. What brings you out and about so early?"

Mrs. Carruthers tucked her purse under her arm and smiled. "The Founder's Day celebration is only a few weeks away. There is much to do and little time in which to do it." She reached up and adjusted the ridiculously large hat sitting upon her head. It was her trademark item of clothing, and she always wore a hat to match her outfit for the day.

Susan nodded her head in agreement. "I'm sure everything will come together just fine. You ladies always put together a lovely celebration for the townsfolk."

"Thank you, my dear. Alice, have you decided?"

Alice Montgomery nodded her white head, the tight curls bouncing as she did so. "I'll take one of those pecan rolls."

Susan bit her lip as both Mrs. Carruthers and Ginny Bolton frowned at her choice. "You really should consider being kinder to your teeth, dear."

Alice rolled her eyes. "I'm going to use them to their full potential while I still have them." She was almost ten years younger than Mrs. Carruthers' seventy-two and Ginny's sixty-nine. And while the other two women had partial dentures, Alice had all of her own teeth and never missed an opportunity to eat things the other two could only dream about now.

Susan listened to their banter and finished placing their selected pastries in individual bags. Once done, the ladies bid her a good day, but not before Mrs. Carruthers offered a bit of friendly advice. "That nice detective who was in here earlier is awfully good-looking. If I were younger, I'd be tempted to go after him myself. You shouldn't let that one get away."

Susan shook her head and didn't answer. Sure, Kip looked like a keeper. But so had her ex back in the big city. And it turned out he was cheating on her with three other women. She wasn't ready to open up again.

Seeing that she had no other customers at the moment, she slipped back into the kitchen and starting sweeping up the broken glass and flour. Mr. Giles was nowhere to be seen, but he'd left his latest treasure lying on the floor. Susan couldn't resist picking it up to have a look.

It was indeed made of metal, brass if she wasn't mistaken, and shaped like a skeleton key from years gone by. She looked at it closely for any markings that might have been etched upon its surface, but there was nothing there. She opened up the glass jar she used to keep Mr. Giles's numerous treasures, at least until their true owners came to claim them, and then she jotted a quick note about his find in her daily journal.

Mr. Giles was a curious cat. As a young kitten he'd gone out carousing only to arrive home the next morning with a token of affection for her. A dead mouse. A piece of jewelry he'd found in the park. A piece of fabric or a hair tie. The list was endless.

As he'd matured, the free-roaming cat become well-known throughout the small town. Weighing in at seventeen pounds, he was a force to be reckoned with, and Susan had allowed him plenty of space to do his thing. Like most cats, he seemed to tolerate most humans, but he only truly showed any kind of real affection to Susan herself.

Meooow!

Susan turned at the plaintive cry and shook her head at Mr. Giles as he stood in the doorway to the kitchen. "You can come back in now. I've cleaned your mess all up."

As if he understood everything she said, he pranced over to her and weaved himself around her legs, purring loudly. Unable to stay upset with the cat, she picked him up and cradled him like a baby. "You're forgiven. And I found the key you brought back with you. Where did you find such a thing? I bet someone is going to come looking for it soon."

Mr. Giles purred even louder, and she scratched his ears before setting him back down on the floor. "We are going on a field trip after work today. Kip came by here and told me that someone robbed a grave last night. I mean, can you imagine? What type of individual has no respect for the dead? I tell you, Mr. Giles, there are some very strange happenings in this town lately. Very strange indeed."

CHAPTER 3

At precisely two o'clock, Susan turned the open sign off and lowered the blinds over the windows. Closing in the early afternoon was one of the perks of getting up at 3:30 a.m. to cook. She went through the display case and covered those items that would last until the next day. She carried the others back into the kitchen and placed them in the appropriate storage space – some in the freezer and some in the refrigerator.

When the dishwasher was loaded for the last time and the floors had been swept and mopped, she turned the lights off in the kitchen and used the back stairs to head to her own apartment. She opened the door and then smiled at the sight that greeted her eyes.

Mr. Giles was spread out on the area rug, purring happily, as he watched her enter.

"Did you have a good day, Mr. Giles?" She quickly changed into a pair of shorts and a t-shirt and grabbed her sneakers. "Ready to go exploring?" she asked the cat when he wandered into the bedroom after her.

Mr. Giles jumped up onto her bed and then sat in the middle of it, blinking his eyes at her in response.

"I wonder whose grave got dug up? And why would anyone want to steal a body?" She kept up a running dialogue as she checked her hair in the mirror. It was still neatly tucked away, nary a hair out of place. She reached for the small tablet and stylus lying on the corner.

"All right, let's go see what kind of mischief occurred at the graveyard last night." She picked up Mr. Giles and then scratched his ears as she headed downstairs. She stepped out the back door and placed him into the large basket on the front of her bike.

Lakeside wasn't a very big town. During the summer months, most of the locals either walked to where they were going, or rode their bikes. As she headed towards the cemetery, she waved at people as she passed them by. The local townsfolk waved back and smiled, but the tourists just looked at her as if she was part of the scenery. She didn't mind. After all, they would be gone within a few days or weeks, most of them never to be seen again.

She arrived at the cemetery and had no trouble finding the scene of the crime. She parked her bike and leaned it against a tree after lifting Mr. Giles down to the freshly cut grass. There was yellow crime scene tape around the disturbed grave, and Susan glanced around the cemetery grounds to see that she was alone. For the moment.

She pulled out her tablet and snapped several photos of the damp ground and the clumps of grass that had been ripped from the area around the headstone. The marble slab was tipped backwards, and she strained to get close enough to see the name and date, but the sun was shining too brightly.

She glanced around one more time and then ducked under the crime tape. She very carefully stepped over to the marble stone. When she saw the name so neatly engraved on the front of the slab, she immediately realized there was more to this crime than Kip had led her to believe.

The grave belonged to Marshall Proctor, the only son of one of the richest families living in Lakeside at the time of his death. The very upper crust Proctor family lived in a large stone house at the end of Main Street. Susan knew very little about the man, or his history, but as she passed her eyes over the scene of the crime, she knew exactly who to ask to rectify that situation. Mrs. Carruthers.

She snapped a few more pictures and then heard a throat being cleared behind her. She looked over her shoulder to see Jeff Baldwin standing just outside the yellow tape, watching her with his knowing eyes.

"Good afternoon, Jeff."

"Susan. Whatcha doin'?" Jeff leaned on the side of the golf cart he used to travel around the cemetery.

"Just checking out the scene of the crime." She quickly ducked back underneath the yellow crime tape and then watched as Mr. Giles sauntered around the new hole in the ground, sniffing curiously here and there. "I don't imagine things like this happen very often."

Jeff slowly shook his head. He was a tall thin man, with thinning hair and a very thin mustache that was barely visible since his once-blond hair was now turning white. His eyes were hidden behind thick glasses and the brim of the baseball cap he always seemed to wear. Having met his wife, she guessed he was in his late fifties, if not his early sixties.

"We don't get much going on at the cemetery. Ever. We've only buried three people this year so far."

Susan nodded her head as she quickly put faces and names to those three individuals. The aging librarian, Sally Stinson. An elderly lady who died three days after celebrating her ninety-fifth birthday, Marge Pauley. And the grandson of Mrs. Carruthers who had been killed while serving overseas. He'd been brought home to be buried in the family plot right next to his great grandparents, Mrs. Carruthers' dearly beloved parents.

"Why do you think someone would want to dig up a grave? Let alone steal the body?" Susan asked.

Jeff shook his head again. "I have no earthly idea. People get themselves some crazy notions these days."

Susan agreed. "That's certainly true. Did you happen to know Mr. Proctor?"

"Well, I can't say that anyone in Lakeside could claim to know Marshall Proctor. I remember him when we were kids. He seemed like a normal enough feller, and then he went off to college. He came back here after his parents passed away, but he kept to himself.

"He very seldom left the house, and had his groceries and other essentials delivered to the back door. I can't imagine living in that huge old house alone for all those years."

Susan had heard rumors about the reclusive man, but she'd never really given him much thought. That was changing now. "All those years? When did he come back to Lakeside?"

"About a decade before he died. He never came back to visit his parents while they were living. Didn't even come home for the funeral when his daddy died. His mama passed away, and a few weeks later Marshall showed back up here."

"Didn't anyone find that strange?" Susan asked.

Jeff shrugged his shoulders. "Some might have. I always thought Marshall was a little off."

Susan was going to ask him to elaborate, but decided to leave further questions for Mrs. Carruthers and her posse of gossips. "The Proctor house never went up for sale, did it?"

"I can't say that I've ever seen a for sale sign there. I don't believe Marshall had any descendants, and I've always wondered why the house was just left sitting there. Some fancy lawyer from Springfield was in charge of the estate."

"Well, I guess I should be getting back to town. I've still got a few errands to run this afternoon. You take care."

Jeff gave her a wink. "You too. I'll be careful not to mention to that man of yours that you was by here."

"Man of mine?" Susan asked cautiously.

"Detective Fletcher. The way my wife told it, you two are dancing around each other and it's only a matter of time before you both get dizzy and crash into each other."

Susan thought she'd been so careful not to wear her heart on her sleeve. Where would Margie have heard such a rumor? "Where did your wife get that idea?"

"Mrs. Carruthers. Who else?"

Who else indeed? That woman thought she knew everything about everything. "Well, I can assure you that Detective Fletcher and I are just friends."

"Whatever you say, Susan. Don't matter none to me."

"Come by the bakery some morning and I'll fix you up with some cinnamon rolls." She turned to look for Mr. Giles. She smiled when she saw that he'd had no qualms about investigating the empty casket. He was sitting on the edge of it, looking very pleased with himself.

"What are you doing, you silly cat? Come along, Mr. Giles. It's time to go home." She gestured for him to come to her. Being the independent feline he was, he proceeded to ignore her and took an interest in cleaning off his front paw.

"You ain't gonna leave him here, are ya?" Jeff asked nervously, eying the big cat.

"Why, I wouldn't think of doing such a thing. I know Mr. Giles is perfectly capable of finding his way back home, but I brought him out here and I'll take him back with me. I'll just slip back inside the tape and get him."

Jeff nodded once and then slid back into his golf cart. "Good. See ya around."

Susan watched him drive off and then she slipped under the crime tape again. She'd only gotten a few pictures of the outside of the casket before Jeff had arrived, and she took this opportunity to snap a few more of the inside.

Mr. Giles was still sitting there calmly bathing his front foot when she reached for him. Before she could grab him, he slipped down inside the casket, laid down, and watched her.

"What's got into you?" she asked him, reaching for him again.

Mr. Giles was being cantankerous and batted at her hand with his claws carefully sheathed. She pulled her hand back and shook a finger at him. "You be nice." She reached for him again, and that's when she noticed a small pink piece of paper sticking up from the satin folds inside the casket.

"What is this?" she asked softly. Shifting Mr. Giles so that she could retrieve the slip of paper, she pulled it free and then turned it over. It appeared to be the corner of something, with two smooth edges and one ragged, torn edge. "Mr. Giles, I do believe you've found a clue."

The pink paper was thick and shiny as if it might have belonged to an advertisement or magazine cover. "This is strange. I wonder how this got in here."

The paper had been wedged down into the casket lining. It either had to have been there when Mr. Proctor was buried-- or the person who dug up his body had left behind a clue.

Meooow!

"Sorry, Mr. Giles." She picked him up, put the piece of paper in her pocket, and headed back to where she'd left her bike. She was playing hard and fast with the law right now, but since Kip was joining her for dinner, she figured she'd give him the piece of paper in person then. *That way if he wants to yell at me for messing with the crime scene, there won't be an audience.*

CHAPTER 4

On her way back into town, she couldn't resist riding her bike by the house where Mr. Proctor had once lived. It was a two-story stone monstrosity that looked completely out of place amid the more modest homes further down the street.

A large stone and wrought iron fence surrounded the large property, with many of its sections showing signs of rusting. The grounds were severely overgrown, with the ivy completely covering the southern side of the house.

The porch was in serious need of painting, and large weeds had grown up in the cracks of the concrete driveway. "Mr. Giles, I don't know who owns this property now, but it's obvious they haven't done a very good job of taking care of it."

She thought it was a shame. She parked her bike and went to the large double gate. The hinges had frozen in place. No matter how hard she pushed, the gate wasn't inclined to budge. She looked around for another way into the property, ignoring the no trespassing signs. She didn't immediately see a way in and was just thinking about trying to squeeze through the fence posts when the sound of a vehicle approaching captured her attention.

She turned and saw Kip pulling his black-and-white to a stop a few feet away from her bike.

"Susan, what are you doing here?" he asked as he got out of his car. "Good afternoon, Mr. Giles." He scratched behind his ears and earned a purr of thanks in return.

"I was just on my way to run a few errands."

"On your way?" Kip looked up the road. "Where were you coming from?"

Susan sighed and let her shoulders droop. "You know where I was coming from. The cemetery."

"I thought I asked you to stop meddling in crime scenes."

"I'm not meddling. I'm helping."

Kip shook his head. Before he could voice his disagreement, she reached into her pocket and pulled the slip of paper out. "I even found a clue. Or rather, Mr. Giles found a clue and then pointed it out to me."

"A clue?" Kip asked, taking the proffered scrap of paper. "What is this?"

"A piece of pink paper."

"I can see that. Where did you find it?"

"Inside the casket. Mr. Proctor's casket."

"You crossed the crime tape?" Kip asked.

"Well, only to snap a few photos. And then Mr. Giles decided the edge of the casket looked like a good place to give himself a bath and…."

Kip raised a hand. "Enough. I've heard enough. You and that cat are going to drive me insane one of these days."

Susan tried to look contrite, but failed miserably. "Admit it. Your investigators missed a crucial piece of evidence."

"A scrap of paper, without any writing on it, is not a crucial piece of evidence."

"What if it belonged to whoever stole the corpse?" she asked with a raised eyebrow.

"What if the wind blew a piece of trash into the casket?"

"No wind today." Susan sighed and then climbed back aboard her bike. "It's okay, you don't have to say thank you."

"Thank you? Why would I…"

"You're welcome. I'll see you later for dinner. Don't forget the meat." Susan pushed off, leaving Kip standing in front of the gates.

Susan stopped by the bakery and deposited Mr. Giles inside the back door. She normally took him everywhere she went, but not the grocery store.

She waved at David Clark, the store manager, as she entered with basket in hand. She'd seen Mrs. Carruthers's car in the parking lot and was hoping to bump into her. She had several questions about Mr. Proctor, and if anyone in Lakeside would know the answers, it was the town gossip.

She headed for the vegetable aisle and was in the process of selecting the makings of a nice salad, when a familiar voice carried to her ears. She glanced up to see Mrs. Carruthers barreling towards her.

"Mrs. Carruthers, imagine seeing you twice in one day."

"Yes, dear. Did you hear about the shenanigans over at the cemetery last night?"

"In fact I did. I went by there earlier this afternoon, just to take a look see…"

She didn't get a chance to finish her sentence before Mrs. Carruthers interrupted her. "Whose grave was it?"

"Marshall Proctor."

"Marshall? I always knew that boy was no good when he came back here and hid himself up in that big mausoleum of a house." She shook her head vigorously, the massive flowers adorning her hat threatening to fly off.

"Did you know Mr. Proctor?" Susan asked.

"Did I know him? Why, of course I did. Such a polite young man in his younger years. But time away from Lakeside changed him."

"Changed him how?"

"He never was the same when he came back here. I asked his mama about him from time to time and she never said much, but I got the impression he'd been a huge disappointment to both of his parents."

"Did you ever find out anything to support that idea?"

"Nothing concrete, but there was a falling out with his father before he died. Marshall didn't even have the courtesy to come home for his daddy's funeral."

His daddy's funeral, Susan thought. *At least his daddy had a funeral.*

"Can you think of anyone who might want to steal his body?"

Mrs. Carruthers shivered. "They stole his body? I hadn't heard that part. Why on earth would anyone want to steal a dead body? Especially one that had been inside a casket for almost six years?"

"I really don't know. Hopefully, Detective Fletcher will be able to find out and catch whoever perpetrated this horrible act."

Mrs. Carruthers nodded her head again. "I'm sure he'll do everything he can. Now, dear, if I might be so bold – you really should consider cooking some of that asparagus to go with your dinner this evening. It looks very fresh, and I'm told that Detective Fletcher is rather fond of that particular vegetable. Have a nice evening."

Susan stared after the older woman with her mouth hanging open. H*ow on earth does she know I'm having dinner with Kip this evening? And how does she know what his favorite vegetable is? I didn't even know that.*

That question continued to bother her as she finished her shopping and headed home.

CHAPTER 5

"So, did you make any headway on that piece of paper I gave you earlier?" Susan asked Kip as they sat on her couch drinking their after-dinner coffees.

"I sent it over to the CSI lab in Springfield. Hopefully, they'll have an answer in a few days."

"I see. So, can you tell me what else was found this morning?"

"You know I'm not supposed to discuss my cases with anyone. And that especially holds true for you. The district attorney almost had my badge after your help on that last murder case."

"I cannot believe how ungrateful he was. Without my assistance, you'd still be looking in the wrong place for the killer."

"I know that, but not everyone is as enamored of your abilities as I am. Especially not Frank."

Susan rolled her eyes and sighed. "Yeah, well, Frank doesn't seem to like me very much."

Frank Matthews was Kip's partner. To him, she was nothing but a busybody playing at being a detective. She could still hear his scathing comments in her mind. *If we weren't so busy saving you from your idiotic schemes, we might actually have time to solve the cases ourselves.*

Frank didn't understand Kip and Susan's bond, which came from their mutual interest in exploring unsolved cases from the 1990-1992 savings and loan scandal. Kip was looking for missing cash. Millions, if not billions, had been written off. There was a wealth of treasure to be found.

But Susan was looking for her father, a loan officer who had vanished at the height of the scandal in 1991-- when she was only four years old. Frank wanted Kip to focus on twenty-first century crimes, but he'd developed a soft spot for the abandoned little girl in Susan's heart.

"So, about the evidence?" Susan asked.

"Nothing," he said. "Aside from that piece of paper you found, we have almost nothing."

"Almost nothing sounds like you might have something."

"A footprint. We have one footprint, evidently left behind by someone in the wee hours of the morning when the ground was still really wet."

"I didn't see any footprint." Susan was already planning another trip back to the cemetery at her first opportunity.

"Don't go back there," Kip said. It was an order.

Susan didn't take orders from men. She changed the subject. "Did you know the man who was buried there?"

"Not very well, I'm afraid. I came to Lakeside about a month before he died. I don't think Proctor got out much."

"From what I hear, he didn't get out at all. Jeff told me he even had his groceries delivered to his house."

"I didn't realize David had a delivery service over at the grocery store."

"Neither did I. Anyway, Jeff said he was different when he came back here, and Mrs. Carruthers seems to think there was some falling out between him and his parents."

Kip shrugged. "Lots of adults fall out with their parents. That's not a crime."

Susan shrugged and scooted a bit closer to him on the couch. "So, have you checked out the house?"

"Why would we? It's been sitting vacant since his death. As you saw earlier, no one's used those front gates in quite some time. There's no reason for us to enter the house. What I really need is a clue as to where the body is being hidden.

"Marshall Proctor wasn't a small man, and hiding a corpse that big might be problematic. Especially considering it would have been hard to carry away from the gravesite."

"I didn't see any tire tracks next to the grave." Susan tried to recall the scene again in her mind.

"I don't recall seeing any either. I'll have to go back over the scene in the morning. For now, how about we find a movie to watch on television that doesn't include murder or crime scene tape?"

Susan handed him the remote. He could pick out the movie, and she would sit next to him on the couch for the next few hours. But in her mind, she was already making a list of things that seemed to require more research.

She cataloged them in her head, placing them in numerical order by their level of importance.

1. *How do you carry off a six-year-old corpse without leaving a trail?*

2. *Where do you hide a six-year-old corpse? Would it still be intact?*

3. *What about the footprint? Did it belong to a male or a female?*

4. *Why Marshall Proctor's grave and not someone else's?*

5. *What was so special about Marshall Proctor after death?*

Kip chose a romantic comedy that she'd seen numerous times before. It was easy to pretend she was watching the movie because she knew most of the classic scenes by heart. At some point, she heard Mr. Giles come in. He sauntered over and jumped up onto the back of the couch, then hopped down, strode over to the large bench window, and began to give himself a bath.

"Mr. Giles seems content this evening," Kip commented as the credits rolled at the end of the movie.

"When does he ever not seem content?" Susan laughed. "If I have a chance to choose my next life, I want to come back as my cat. He comes and goes as he pleases, eats whenever he wants, and no one even thinks twice about being snubbed by him."

"Mr. Giles does seem to have it made. Well." Kip stood up and stretched his arms over his head. "I should probably head home. Tomorrow looks like it's going to be a busy day."

Susan walked with him to the back door of her apartment. A small patio led to a staircase at the rear of the building, providing direct access to the apartment without having to enter the bakery below. "Thank you for the steaks. They were delicious."

"Thank you for cooking them so well. And the salad and asparagus were very nice complements to the meat. My thanks to the chef."

"Your appreciation is noted." It was an awkward moment. Kip was a great guy, but...

Kip hugged her closer. But maybe he felt the sudden tension in her shoulders. His kiss landed at the corner of her mouth for only a brief moment before he pulled away. "Sleep well tonight. I'd tell you to stay away from the cemetery, but I'd be wasting my breath."

She nodded her head into his chest and said nothing.

He sighed. "Well, just don't tamper with anything else that appears to be evidence."

Susan forced herself to smile. "I promise. Next time I find a clue your team left behind, I'll call you and have you come collect it."

"You do that. Goodnight." He hesitated.

For a moment, Susan wondered if he'd try for a kiss again. But instead he let himself out the door. She could hear him pause outside to listen for the lock clicking into place. At last she heard him walk down the creaky stairs.

CHAPTER 6

Susan gazed out the window, watching as the lights inside the nearby houses slowly flickered out. It was almost midnight when Mr. Giles began to stir in her lap, sitting up and turning his attention out the window too.

When the slow steadiness of his purr was interrupted by a low growl, Susan perked up from her near catatonic state to rub his ears. "What's wrong, Mr. Giles?"

His attention was fixed out the window. She scanned the street below, but nothing seemed amiss. She had extinguished all of the lights in her living room except for a small string of blue accent lights hung across the electric fireplace set in the adjacent wall. She hadn't bothered to close the curtains in the bay window, and she slowly let her eyes scan the entire town looking for what had captured her cat's attention.

In the far distance, she thought she saw the glimmer of a light high up in the trees. As quickly as it appeared, it vanished.

"What was that?" she whispered to the cat who was now sitting at attention and gazing out the window.

She watched for the light to re-appear, but after thirty minutes, she decided she must be more tired than she thought. Glancing at the clock, she realized she had to be awake and in the kitchen in less than three hours. "Time for bed. I'm definitely going to need a nap tomorrow afternoon." She picked up the cat and carried him to her bedroom.

Mr. Giles purred loudly. Susan set him on the left side of the four poster bed and then readied herself for sleep. She took out her hair, letting it fall over her shoulders as she gave it the requisite one hundred brush strokes the way her grandmother taught her.

When it was tangle-free and shining, she pulled it into a low ponytail and settled herself amidst the sheets. "Goodnight, Mr. Giles." She felt the cat move higher up on the bed, taking up his normal position on the covers, as she closed her eyes and let sleep claim her.

Her dreams were filled with snapshots of the crime scene, pictures of the open grave and empty casket, and images of the old stone house. The piece of pink paper flitted in and out of her mind. As she slept, her subconscious began to formulate a plan to help attain some answers to the crime. Susan Becker might not have her investigator's license, but her mind was on the trail and she was determined to help the authorities however she could. Whether they appreciated it or not.

An empty casket. Her own father didn't even have that much. The authorities didn't solve every crime. Too often, they just gave up.

Susan would never give up.

*****

When her alarm went off two and a half hours later, she rolled over and groaned loudly. She blinked the sleep from her eyes and then pushed herself up in the bed. She glanced over to see Mr. Giles still sleeping soundly and wished that for once she could simply roll over and go back to sleep. But the bakery needed fresh merchandise to sell, and that meant she needed to get downstairs and start the ovens.

Twenty minutes later, she was in the kitchen, yawning as she mixed up the ingredients for cinnamon rolls. While the dough was rising, she started the batter for the doughnuts and started warming up the oil in the deep fryer.

She glanced at the calendar in passing and then groaned. Tomorrow evening she was supposed to have five of her special strawberry layer cakes ready for a birthday party being held by a group of tourists staying on one of the houseboats moored on the lake.

She quickly took stock of the ingredients in the refrigerator and realized that her afternoon nap would have to be postponed until after she'd made another grocery run. The cream cheese filling in her specialty cake couldn't happen without the cream cheese.

Three hours later, she was pulling the last pan of rolls from the ovens and drizzling her famous caramel topping over the top. She washed her hands and then headed to the display cases. She loaded her goods onto the proper plates and then flipped the open sign on. It was Thursday, and that meant the morning would more than likely be slow until around eight o'clock.

She started a fresh pot of coffee and then poured herself a cup, adding ample sugar and milk to help cover up the bitter taste. She really didn't like the stuff, but she craved the caffeine. This morning more than most, she needed a good jolt to keep going.

Around eight, the first groups of tourists began filtering in, looking for a quick breakfast before they headed out for a day on the lake. Her bakery was right on the way to the boat docks, and since Lakeside didn't have any fast food restaurants to boast about, a quick stop by the local bakery became the next best thing.

She kept her ears peeled for any mention of the strange light she'd seen the night before. Several of the tourists did mention it.

It was coming from that old abandoned house. I hear there's a ghost living there. He must be getting restless.

Susan couldn't resist adding to their story. "How do you know the ghost isn't a woman?"

That got quite a reaction, and they left discussing the new female ghost that was haunting the town of Lakeside. Susan could only laugh at how easily these summer people believed nonsense.

Around eleven, a couple in their forties or fifties came in. The gentleman was surly and looked like he hadn't slept enough in several nights. The woman had carefully applied makeup to cover up the dark circles beneath her eyes. When Susan took their order, she was shocked to notice how dirty the man's fingernails were.

Most of the tourists who visited Lakeside were on the wealthier side. Seeing someone with hands that looked like they had been hard at work recently seemed very odd to her.

"So, you folks up here for vacation?" Susan asked while she waited for the coffee to finish brewing.

The man turned away, but the woman stepped forward. "Just for a few days."

"So, where are you from?" Susan asked.

"Chicago."

"Big city. Quite a bit of a change from here in Lakeside," Susan said.

"Yes, it is much quieter here than back home."

Susan finished filling their coffee cups and handed them across the display case, only to watch the woman's cup slip from her shaky hands, drop to the tiled floor, and splash everywhere.

"Oh my! Are you okay?" Susan grabbed for a rag and hurried around the counter.

The woman's reflexes had saved her from a nasty burn, but her shoes were soaked with the brown liquid. As she scooted backwards, she left muddy footprints in her wake. The tracks were very distinctive, leaving tread marks as well as a perfectly shaped outline of a heart in the center of each heel. Susan passed the woman one of the towels.

"I'm so sorry."

"Don't be. My hands are just a little shaky this morning, and it was entirely my fault."

"Why don't you sit down and wipe your legs off and I'll get you a damp cloth as well as another cup of coffee?"

The woman smiled at her, but her companion seemed angry. The scowl on his face deepened. As Susan headed back around the counter to wet a towel with water, she saw him whisper something into the woman's ear that had her shaking her head agitatedly. She shushed him when she saw they were being watched.

She offered Susan a weak smile and then averted her eyes.

"Here you go." Susan handed her a wet cloth and another cup of coffee. "Are you sure you're not burned?"

"I'm fine. My shoes were in need of a good washing anyway. I'm so sorry about your floor and the mess."

"Don't worry about it. I normally sweep and mop at the end of the day, so today I'll just get to it a little earlier than normal. Don't give it another thought."

"If you're sure?" the woman asked.

"I'm positive." Susan retrieved their chosen muffins and watched as they both left the bakery, walking hurriedly towards a truck with most of the windows completely blacked out. Shaking her head, she retrieved the mop bucket and began cleaning up the mess.

She was once again struck by the strange tread marks the woman's shoes had left. *How much do you pay for shoes that leave such a distinctive mark? Those are definitely designer and not something you'd find around here.*

By the time she'd cleaned up the front floors and dealt with the inventory, she was yawning repeatedly and in dire need of a nap. Deciding to close up just a few minutes early, she turned the sign off and cleaned up the kitchen. She dragged herself upstairs to her apartment, where Mr. Giles greeted her at the door.

When he weaved himself around her legs, she realized that she'd forgotten to leave him a plate of food this morning, and she was surprised he hadn't come to the kitchen to remind her of her failure. When she glanced towards the patio door, she realized that the poor cat hadn't been able to leave the apartment, since the wind had blown an empty pot in front of the pet door, preventing it from being pushed open.

"Sorry, Mr. Giles. Hope about a nice can of tuna to make up for my lapse?" She pulled the can from the pantry and smiled as the cat jumped up onto the counter to see. A plaintive cry let her know he approved of her choice and that she wasn't moving fast enough to put it on the plate.

"Here you go, spoiled cat." Susan threw the empty can away and then ran a hand down his back. Stifling another yawn, she shook her head. "I know I have things to do, but first a small nap." She unblocked the patio door and then headed for the bedroom. She quickly removed the pins from her neat hair bun, leaving the ponytail holder in, and fell into her bed. She pulled a thin sheet up to her neck and then closed her eyes in a sigh of contentment.

"This is the best part of this day." Within minutes, she was fast asleep.

CHAPTER 7

Susan stretched and then came abruptly awake. *What time is it?* She glanced at the clock sitting next to her bed and realized that she'd slept the entire afternoon away. A knocking on her patio door had her hurrying from the bed to see who had come calling at…eight o'clock at night?

Kip stood on the small deck, looking very worried. She opened the door just as he was getting ready to knock again. "Hi."

"Why aren't you answering your phone?" he asked, stepping inside her small apartment.

Susan arched her back as she stretched her tired muscles. "I fell asleep. Did you need something?"

"I've been trying to get hold of you all afternoon. The lab got back to me on that scrap of paper you found. It's from a recent issue of a popular women's magazine."

"Really? How are they so certain?"

"The color is an identical match, as is the paper content and chemical composition of the ink used during the printing process."

"Wow! I guess I never imagined your grave robber as being a woman."

Kip grabbed a bottle of water from her fridge and then seated himself on her couch. "If the grave robber was a woman, she wasn't acting alone. There's no way a woman could move that corpse without help. According to the coroner's report, Marshall Proctor weighed two hundred and thirty pounds at the time of his death."

No woman could lift a dead corpse weighing that much. "So, do you, or don't you, believe you're looking for a woman?"

Kip sighed. "I really don't know. I did check with David over at the grocery store, and he doesn't carry this particular magazine. And it's from the most recent issue. Guess we're looking for a tourist."

Great! Like there aren't hundreds of them running around town. "So, what is your plan now?"

"I don't know that I have one."

Susan bit her lip and her mind was suddenly wide awake. *Well, if you don't have a plan, I certainly do. I'm going to figure out who would want to steal Marshall Proctor's body.*

"Do you want something to eat?" she asked as she headed for the small efficiency kitchen.

"No, I just wanted to make sure you were okay. I saw Mr. Giles down at the city park and when I couldn't get hold of you, I came over."

"Thanks for checking up on me, but I didn't get much sleep last night and fell asleep right after I came up here."

Kip pushed himself off the couch and headed for the patio door. "Well, I'll get out of your hair. Call me tomorrow?"

Susan nodded, hiding a yawn behind her hand. "I will. Goodnight."

Susan fried herself an egg and toasted a slice of bread for dinner. She ate and then cleaned up the kitchen, glancing at the patio door several times as she did so. Mr. Giles had yet to come back. As the clock reached ten o'clock and then eleven, she found herself drifting off while sitting on the couch.

She took a pad and a pencil and began making a list for herself. Tomorrow after work, she would visit the local library and see what sort of information she could come up with concerning Marshall Proctor, and the Proctor family in general.

When she began yawning non-stop, she put the pencil down and realized she'd done all she could for the day. Making sure the patio door was unblocked, she headed back to bed. She was counting the days until Sunday, looking forward to being able to sleep in for two whole days without having to get up and be in the kitchen in the wee hours of the night.

*****

She was awakened by Mr. Giles jumping up onto the bed around midnight, and she immediately realized that the cat was soaking wet. She turned the lamp on and surveyed her best friend. He was licking himself furiously in a hopeless attempt to remove the water.

"What happened to you?" she asked, retrieving a towel from the bathroom and wrapping him up for a few minutes. Mr. Giles struggled to get out, but she kept rubbing anyway. For his own health, he needed to be dried off-- and fast.

She tossed the towel into the dirty hamper and then padded over to the window, expecting to see it raining profusely outside. It was dry. "So where did you come into contact with all sorts of water tonight?"

She eyed the cat who was doing his best to look totally offended that his gray fur coat had gotten wet. She chuckled as he continued to try and clean himself up, and then she returned to bed. "Well, I don't know how you got all wet, but whatever happened, I bet you don't go there again."

She turned the light off and tuned out the cat's soft, self-pitying cries. He was mostly dry now. He'd be fine. She'd find out how he got so wet tomorrow.

*****

The answer came when she entered her kitchen to start the morning chores. She went to fill a large pot with water so that she could boil it for the pretzels, but only a few drips came from the faucet.

Exasperated, she closed her eyes and counted to ten. *Guess I know a possible reason Mr. Giles was all wet.*

She opened the back door and then immediately shut it again. There was water running down the street in a small river heading towards the lake. She went to the front of the store, but the water was running all the way down Main Street. She couldn't quite tell where it was coming from.

Well, guess I get to go for a walk this morning. The wind was starting up, and she wasn't quite sure, but she thought the sky was filled with clouds. At four o'clock in the morning, and on a moonless night, it was awfully hard to tell.

She grabbed a flashlight, but when she went to turn it on, she remembered that it needed new batteries. The weak light coming from the lamp would do her absolutely no good. Her cell phone would have to do for a source of light. Once outside, she saw Mr. Giles watching her from the bedroom window above.

She started down the sidewalk, intent on finding the source of the water break so that she could call it in and get a repair crew headed this way. It was Friday, and early enough that no other businesses or homes seemed to be stirring.

She should phone it in first. She knew that. But what if someone was trying to wash away a crime?

The authorities didn't always figure things out. They lost time. And lost time sometimes meant you never solved the mystery.

She'd check it out herself. And then she'd call.

CHAPTER 8

The water seemed to be increasing in volume as she began her walk along the second block. It was now running down the middle of the road, instead of following the curb and gutter system at the side. She reached the end of the street and paused when she saw where the water was coming from. The Proctor house.

Water was rushing from beneath and around the wrought iron gates, and it appeared to be coming from the rear of the large house. The concrete drive was roiling with muddy water, and she hurried across the street, walking down the left hand side of the fence as she looked for a way in.

About fifty yards down, she found two of the iron poles had collapsed, providing ample room for her to fit through. She bent her knees and quickly slid through the opening sideways, smiling at how easy that had been.

I wonder why no one else has done that? She figured the allure of the big empty house would have tempted some of the local teens, and maybe even a summer visitor or two to trespass. She ignored the little voice in her head that said she was doing the same thing. She wasn't trespassing so much as performing a public service to the community at large.

If the water break originated on the Proctor property, the repair crew would need to know that. And she wanted to be sure of her facts before she called it in.

She followed the small river of water around the left side of the house, shivering as the wind picked up. An owl hooted overhead. She was thankful there wasn't a moon this early in the morning. She was having a hard enough time dealing with the overgrown brush around the house. She definitely didn't need any creepy shadows from the massive oak trees messing with her mind as well.

She reached the corner of the house and prepared to follow the water into the back yard, but she couldn't go any further without walking into the moving water. All of her childhood warnings came rushing back at her. Stories about cottonmouths. Stories about sinkholes. Stories about people being swept away in a flood and not being found for weeks...

The small river was almost ten feet across now. From where she stood, she figured it was probably a good three to four inches deep as it gushed from the back yard. She shouldn't do what she was thinking. She really shouldn't. It was insanity.

And yet what else could she do? What caused those pipes to break, tonight, at the home of a man whose corpse had been stolen? Was somebody deliberately destroying all evidence of his life? She thought about her missing father once again.

Maybe he'd stolen the money. Maybe he was on the track of the person who had really stolen it. Nobody knew. She couldn't seem to get closure.

She couldn't sit back and let another set of criminals get away with... with what? She didn't even know.

She had to find out.

Rising to her full height, she took another step, and then another until she had reached the side of the house. She could feel the concrete walk under her feet and she slowly made her way through the muddy water to find the source of the flood. As she reached the middle of the backyard, she could see that it seemed to be coming from the top of a small hill about sixty feet from the rear of the house.

She walked along the edge of the water, goosebumps rising on her arms thanks to the wind.

She reached the small rise and stopped. A gaping hole in the overgrown lawn was now filled with bubbling, frothing water as it gushed from the pipes underground to the surface.

She pulled out her cell phone and dialed the twenty-four hour emergency line. She told the dispatcher what was happening and gave them directions to the house. When they asked about access, she had to tell them that the house was abandoned and that there was a locked gate at the front.

The dispatcher didn't seem to think that would be a problem and promised that they would be there just as soon as a repair crew could be mobilized. Susan thanked her and then headed back to the small patio at the back of the house.

The brick flooring was overgrown with weeds, but she managed to find a spot near the built-in hearth to seat herself. *I need to put up a sign in the window saying we're closed today. Without water, there is no way I can cook or clean up.* She glanced at her watch, and then relaxed slightly. It was going on five a.m. but she wasn't supposed to open until at least six; she had plenty of time to walk back to the bakery and take care of business.

I'll just wait until they get the water stopped and then leave.

It only took ten minutes. She was impressed by the speed with which the water had been shut off. There was only one person in town who actively worked for the water company, and she figured he must have gotten a call to turn off the main water valve. Miles Hanson was also her helper Julie's father, as well as the current mayor. Susan caught her breath and hurried around front to meet him. As she slipped onto the street side of the property, she realized sunrise was only a few minutes away.

The sky was already taking on the eerie white that happens just before the burst of colors appear. She stood there for a few minutes, watching the rising sun illuminate the rosy clouds that were moving quickly across the sky.

She was still staring up when she heard an approaching vehicle. It was Kip's black-and-white, and she mentally cringed at the lecture she was sure to receive. It was especially embarrassing because she could see that Miles was with him.

She reached a hand up to her hair, glad that she'd taken time to twist it up onto the top of her head before entering the kitchen this morning. She glanced down and saw that her tennis shoes were absolutely caked with the red Missouri mud. So were her legs up to her knees, with splatters dotting her clothing above that.

"Suzie, what in the world are you doing out here this time of the morning?" Kip asked as he exited his car.

"I got up to start baking and didn't have any water. I didn't want to call it in before I knew where the break was, so I followed the water to here." It sounded lame even in her own ears.

"And you're positive the water is coming from the back of the house?" Miles surveyed the closed gate with a frown upon his face.

She pointed to the left. "There was a hole in the fence down there. I slipped through and then followed the water until I reached the source of the break. By the way, Miles, good morning."

"Morning, unfortunately I'm not seeing the good side to this right now. The main water line coming into town is what appears to be broken. You're going to be out of water all day, and maybe even tomorrow."

Susan thought of all the things she could get done if the bakery was forced to be closed down until next week. She would lose some revenue, but she could also get a lot of questions answered about the Proctors. Marshall didn't seem to have any family left. Fine. It was up to Susan to make sure that whoever stole his corpse was going to pay.

"Say, I'm going to slip through that fence opening and go take a look around," Miles said.

"Be careful. In order to get to the back of the house you'll have to walk through the muddy water." Susan felt Kip's stare, but she ignored it as best she could. She knew walking through the water hadn't been smart, but she didn't need Kip to tell her so.

She was twenty-eight years old. Kip was thirty-five, and a seven year age difference didn't give him the right to lecture her. She was a grown woman capable of deciding for herself when to take a chance.

"I could come with you, if you like?" Susan offered.

Kip stopped her from following the other man with a hand on her arm. "Why don't I drive you home instead? I assume you need to put up a closed sign in the window? Miles, I'll swing back by here and grab you after I drop her off."

"Don't bother," Miles said. "The work crew will be here shortly. I'll check out the damage and then work on getting that gate opened up. If I don't succeed, we'll be forced to tear it off."

"Understood." Kip turned back to Susan. "Ready to go?" "In fact, I am. Thank you. I would love to accept your kind offer. My tennis shoes are wet and already beginning to rub on my ankles."

He spread a plastic raincoat over the passenger side seat in an attempt to keep the mud from getting everywhere. For the moment, he didn't say another word.

CHAPTER 9

Probably waiting until he has me alone in the car to lecture me on trespassing. She sighed, but slid into the passenger seat.

Since Main Street was flooded with dirty water, he turned the sedan around and took the side streets as he navigated his way back to her bakery. "You do realize how dangerous it was for you to search out the problem on your own, right?"

"It didn't feel dangerous. I wanted the repair crew to know what they were getting into."

"That's their job, not yours. What if there had been a sinkhole under all of that water you walked through? You know that's not something you're supposed to do around here."

Susan nodded her head slowly. "I know. It did flash through my mind, but then I figured it was worth the risk."

"No, it wasn't. You know it wasn't."

Susan decided not to argue the point with him, since they were now in front of the bakery. "Thank you for the ride."

"No problem. So, what are you going to do with this unexpected day off? Sleep?"

"No, I thought I'd make a trip to the library." *They have copies of all the old newspapers. I'm going to find out as much as I can about the Proctor family today.*

"Ah, getting a good book to read. I used to love sitting in front of the fire reading at night. Doesn't get to happen too often nowadays, but I still enjoy it from time to time. Pick out something good."

"I'll do that. Thank you again for the ride." She glanced down at her muddy shoes. "I think I'll need to figure out a way to clean up without water today too."

Kip glanced at her feet. "Those shoes are never coming clean again."

"Yeah, I know. Guess these just became my new spelunking shoes."

"How many pairs does that make now?"

"More than I can wear out in a lifetime. See ya later."

Inside the bakery, she slipped her muddy shoes off and put them into a pastry bag so that she wouldn't get the floors all dirty. She wiped her feet off with some paper towels and then cleaned up the floor to remove all traces of her muddy footprints.

After affixing a sign to the front door, she threw the locks and headed to the apartment, her mind already busy making a list of questions she wanted to find answers to.

Mr. Giles was waiting. Once again, she saw that the empty pot had blown over and was blocking the pet door and his freedom.

"Sorry, Mr. Giles. I'll find another place to store that pot today. I promise." She set the pot back into its rightful place, but Mr. Giles was more intent on securing his breakfast than he was in taking a morning stroll.

She poured some kibble into his bowl and opened a can of wet food, placing it on a plate before setting it on the ground in front of the cat. He immediately began lapping up the juices, and she smiled at how easily satisfied he was.

Meoow!

Susan reached down and picked up Mr. Giles. "There was a water break on the Proctor estate. That's where all of the water came from. Let me clean up a bit, and then we'll take a walk down there and see if the repair crew has arrived yet."

She set the cat down and reached for the twenty gallons of emergency water she always kept in the apartment. She put the stopper into the sink drain and poured some of the water into the basin. She wet a washcloth and then started with her face, working her way down to her muddy feet. She had to change the water out twice, but by the time she was finished, she felt much readier to face the day.

*****

When Susan, with Mr. Giles following close behind her, arrived back at the Proctor estate, she was pleased to see that they'd been able to open the gates without pulling them off. The flow of water had ceased, and now a muddy trail was all that remained.

She could hear repair men working in the rear of the house, but she detoured to the front porch instead. Her curiosity about the house was getting the better of her, and she was dying to see inside. She looked through the windows, frowning because most of them were covered by curtains.

On a whim, she stepped to the front door and tried the handle, smiling gleefully when it turned in her hand.

She glanced around to see if anyone had noticed and then slipped inside the old house, waiting for Mr. Giles to clear the door before quickly shutting it again. *I can't believe the door was unlocked. I wonder how long it's been like that? Probably since Marshall died so many years ago.*

A thick layer of dust covered everything, including the wooden floors where she walked. She glanced down to see if she was leaving a trail, and that's when she noticed the myriad of other footprints in the dust laden floor.

"Well, Mr. Giles. It seems we are not the only ones curious about the inside of this house." She saw that the footprints seemed to move into every room, including up the wide wooden staircase. "Let's check out this floor first." Her companion happily followed her as she made her way to the back of the house.

She passed a formal dining room and then found herself entering a cook's dream kitchen. Even though the house was older, the kitchen was amazing. Large double ovens occupied the far wall, and a huge island with a dark green marble counter top sat in the center. The space was easily twice the kitchen she had at the bakery. She could only imagine having this much space to work in.

She reached the windows and stopped to watch the workmen out back. They had a small backhoe and had dug a trench from the small rise and down towards the patio. A piece of broken pipe lay to the side, and a new pipe was currently lying nearby, ready to be installed at the earliest opportunity.

She turned, ready to explore the remainder of the house, when something lying on the floor captured her attention. As she bent over to pick it up, she felt her heart beat a little faster. *A magazine. A pink magazine, missing the corner.*

Susan was so excited about her find that she picked it up before remembering her promise to Kip. *I said I wouldn't disturb any more evidence. Well, that promise went out the window.* She put the magazine back down where she'd found it and withdrew her cellphone from her pocket.

"Kip? It's Susan."

"Suzie, where are you? I just stopped by the bakery and you obviously are not at home."

"Uhm…well…I'm at the Proctor estate, and I found something I think you need to see."

"Why are you back at the Proctor estate?" he asked with an exasperated sigh.

"Well, Mr. Giles and I were heading to the library, and I thought I would stop by and see if the repairmen knew how long it might be before the town had its water back."

"And did you get an answer?" he asked.

"Well, from the window I could see that they have the broken pipe already removed."

"Window?! Please tell me you didn't break into the Proctor house."

"I didn't have to break in. The front door was unlocked."

Her statement was met with a long moment of silence. "Stay right there and don't touch anything else," Kip finally said. "Frank and I are on our way."

CHAPTER 10

Of course, Susan didn't heed his advice. "Mr. Giles, we should take a look upstairs. Detective Fletcher is on his way, and if we don't see the house now, we're probably not going to get another chance."

Susan had no doubt in her mind that Kip would be locking down the house after this incident, and that would mean no more unauthorized field trips inside. She started up the winding staircase, then paused as a thought occurred to her.

What if the owner of that magazine is still in the house? It's obvious they were at the gravesite. What if whoever that magazine belongs to stole Marshall's body?

Mr. Giles didn't seem to have any fears. He skirted around her legs to bound up the stairs. At the top, he turned and looked at her, his green eyes blinking before he took off down the right hallway.

"Mr. Giles," she whispered loudly. "Come back here." She followed the cat, hoping she wasn't headed for danger. Then she felt a breeze against the back of her legs and heard the front door close.

"Susan?" Kip saw her at the top of the stairs as she turned around to greet him. "I thought I told you to stay put and not go exploring in here."

"I just wanted to see what the rest of the house looked like. Besides, Mr. Giles came up here, and I need to retrieve him."

Kip gestured for her to come down. "We'll worry about Mr. Giles later. Now, putting aside the fact that you entered this property without authorization, what did you find?"

Susan reached the ground floor. "You're not going to believe it."

"Probably not, but show me anyway."

Susan led him back to the kitchen, pointing out the magazine on the floor. "There. It's the perfect match for that piece of paper I found in the casket."

Kip looked at the magazine and then at the disturbed dust around it. "Tell me you didn't pick it up."

Susan shrugged. "Can't. But I did put it right back where I found it. Doesn't that count for something?"

"Yeah, something." He withdrew a pair of gloves from his jacket pocket and then carefully picked up the magazine, noticing the torn corner on the front and agreeing with her that it was a perfect match. "I'll get this to the lab, but I'm guessing the piece of paper we found will be an exact match for this missing corner."

Susan glanced around. "Where is Frank?" She wasn't overly fond of Kip's partner, but she always tried to be polite whenever she saw him.

"He's outside doing some checking around. Let's go get Mr. Giles and get out of here. I'll have a forensics team come up from Springfield and do a thorough search of the premises. Probably won't happen until tomorrow, but if there's more evidence to find here, we'll find it."

Susan wanted to suggest they perform an initial search, but she knew that wouldn't go over well. She headed back to the stairs, hoping Mr. Giles wasn't going to play a spontaneous game of hide and seek. Kip didn't appear to have that much patience this morning.

The front door opened, and Frank came walking in. "Hey, we've got to go. There's a problem down at the docks. Evidently some speed boat cut off a water skier, cutting the lines and almost drowning the kid out on the water. The father wasn't happy and followed the speed boat back to the docks. His fists somehow ended up in the driver's face, and an all-out brawl ensued. They need every hand available down there to sort things out."

Kip was torn – he needed to get Susan out of the house, but that required finding her cat. And he really needed to be down at the docks. Turning to her, he said, "Promise me you'll grab Mr. Giles and get out of here. I'll come by later, and we can talk some more."

Susan nodded her head. "I'll get him and be gone. Good luck getting everything settled down."

"Thanks."

She watched as the two men turned to leave, smiling at Frank's question.

"Does she take that cat everywhere with her?"

She didn't hear Kip's answer, but it didn't matter. She did take Mr. Giles with her most places because she'd learned early on that if she left him at home, he would escape at the first opportunity. Better to know he was with her than to wonder what trouble he was getting into.

She climbed the stairs and began a methodical check of the various rooms. Mr. Giles had left dainty little footprints in the deeper patches of dust, and she eventually found him sitting in a bay window much like the one at home.

"What are you doing in here, Mr. Giles?" she asked, joining him at the dusty window.

She could see the repairmen hard at work. As she scanned the rest of the estate, dark patches of earth caught her attention. They appeared to be piles of freshly dug up dirt that stood out among the rest of the property because they were devoid of weeds.

She counted almost fifteen such sites, but it was the one furthest from the house that really captured her attention. It was much bigger than the rest. Her curiosity once again flared to life. "Let's take a little detour on the way home. Shall we?"

Once the repair crew had the new pipe in place, they'd want to investigate the source of the break. They'd surely be interested in the evidence of all this illegal digging on the property. Susan would like to see it first. They'd just be trying to find out who to give the ticket to. She was trying to find a missing corpse. Who was really the most motivated to do a thorough investigation?

She picked up the cat and headed for the downstairs. If she was right, she could walk out the back door and just keep walking straight until she reached the new pile of dirt. The repairmen didn't pay her any mind at all when she stepped from the house, and she continued on her way.

She kept hold of Mr. Giles, even though he tried to get down. The weeds were much taller than her five feet six, and if she were to lose sight of him here, she'd have a horrible time locating him again.

A wild raspberry plant blocked her path entirely at one point, the vicious little thorns along its stems biting into her hands as she carefully lifted the vines to allow her to pass. Twenty minutes after leaving the house, she walked out into a small clearing to see the large pile of dirt sitting there. It was obvious that something had either been dug up or buried there. She looked around and wasn't surprised in the least to find a shovel leaning against a nearby bush.

She set Mr. Giles down. "Stay right here. There's no telling what kind of pickle you'll get into if you get tangled up in these weeds."

She grabbed the shovel and then began to slowly clear the soft dirt away from the corner closest to her. She dug slowly and carefully until she encountered something very unlike dirt.

She probed with the shovel for a moment to brush the dirt away from the object. A shoe. She cleared the dirt away from the other side of the soft dirt and encountered another identical shoe.

She stood up and quickly called Kip's phone.

"Suzie, what's up? Did you have any trouble finding Mr. Giles?"

"No, Mr. Giles is right here with me. Now, before you start lecturing me, I only did what any great detective would do. I followed the leads."

Kip sighed dramatically. "What did you find?"

"A body? Maybe? Most definitely a pair of shoes that are definitely attached to ankles."

"You found a body? Where?"

"Buried at the back of the property."

"I don't have time for a full rundown right now. Go back to the bakery and wait for me there. I'll come get you as soon as I can and you can show me where you found this body."

"That's fine." Susan really had no desire to unearth a corpse, either a recent one or a six-year-old one. While she loved finding clues, finding dead bodies was definitely something she could leave to the professionals.

CHAPTER 11

She made a slight detour by the library on her way home. They had a sign in the window reminding people there were no restrooms available, but everyone was welcome to come inside anyway. Since it was one of the few places still open to the public, a variety of people had ventured inside the small building looking for something to entertain themselves with.

Susan headed directly for the newspaper room. After a brief discussion with Missy, the librarian, she was sitting in front of a stack of newspapers. She leafed through them for articles about the Proctor family. Mr. Proctor had been an investment banker at one time, but a combination of bad luck and poor investment choices had completely destroyed the family fortune in the end.

When he'd died, his healthy life insurance policy was the only thing that had prevented the bank from foreclosing on the Lakeside house. The five million dollar policy had been used to pay off everything and still left a nice sum in the bank for Mrs. Proctor to live out the rest of her life.

She sorted through the papers until she found the issue containing the death notice for Mrs. Proctor. It was very basic and didn't contain much personal information at all. It almost looked like it could have been put together using readily available public information. Very insensitive. She searched the following weeks, but couldn't find any trace of an obituary.

Missy was walking by, and Susan gestured her over. "I can't seem to find an obituary for the late Mrs. Proctor."

"That's because there wasn't one. The coroner's office pieced together a death notice for the paper, but no one ever submitted an obituary for her."

"Not even the son?"

Missy shook her head. "No. He didn't show up here until several weeks after her death. Personally, I don't think the attorney handling the estate had an easy time finding him."

Susan thought a moment. "What about Mr. Proctor? Was an obituary ever submitted for him?"

Missy smiled. "Oh yes. Mrs. Proctor submitted it herself. My daddy ran the press back then, and he often told stories of how she came into the newspaper office two days after his death and paid for a full page to be printed about her late husband."

Susan sorted through the papers until she found the correct one. "I found it."

"Good. Let me know if there's anything else you need."

Susan nodded her head as she began to read a synopsis of the elder Mr. Proctor's life. She read about his early childhood and his education. She read about the various cities he'd lived in, and how he and his wife had only been blessed with one child. A son they had named Marshall.

She was about to give up hope of finding anything useful, when something at the end of the obituary caught her attention. In the last paragraph, there was a list of his survivors.

He leaves behind a loving wife, Rose, of Lakeside, Missouri and one son, Marshall (Patricia), of Chicago, Illinois.

Susan felt her heart pick up speed. She waved at Missy, pointed to the paper, and asked her, "What does that look like to you?"

Missy read the last part of the obituary and then looked perplexed. "Well, that's how you normally indicate the name of a person's spouse. But Marshall Proctor wasn't married."

"Are you sure? According to the obituary his mother submitted, it looks like he was. At least, at the time of his father's death."

Missy shrugged. "That must have been a mistake or something. If Marshall Proctor had been married, I'm sure the rest of the town would have heard about it. Or at least, someone would have come forward to collect the estate he left behind when he died."

Susan thanked the woman. One of the library computers was currently vacant. Unable to leave a mystery alone, she logged onto the Illinois public information system and did a name search under marriage licenses for Marshall Proctor. She would have had to pay for a public records search if she did it on her phone, but the library already had a subscription to the service.

When the screen refreshed and his name appeared under the found records, she clicked on the link, biting her lip as she waited for confirmation that the newspaper had been printed correctly. The record came up and she was pleased to see that Marshall Proctor was married to Patricia Jahnke five years prior to his father's death. *Five years and no one in the town had been the wiser. Why?*

She started to close down the system, but then stopped and did another complete records search for both individuals. Marshall Proctor. Patricia Jahnke. And Patricia Proctor. The search took longer this time, and what appeared on the screen caused her to scramble for pencil and paper.

In addition to the marriage record, there was also a record of a divorce order under Marshall's name. Those were the only records tied directly to him-- but not to his wife. She had a variety of records, most of them coming from the court system.

Patricia Proctor had been arrested for robbing a bank two weeks before Marshall's father had passed away. The trial had taken place eighteen months later, due no doubt to the backlog of cases in the large city of Chicago, and she'd been found guilty. Well, Patricia Jahnke had been found guilty. The divorce order was dated for nine days before her trial had ended. It seemed Marshall hadn't been willing to stick by his criminal wife.

She looked at the dates again and was shocked to discover that his mother had passed away before the trial was over. *Had she even known what her son was going through?* Susan was no

CHAPTER 13

Susan couldn't sleep. Mr. Giles had yet to come home, but that wasn't what was worrying her. Every time she closed her eyes, she saw the small piles of freshly dug dirt in the Proctor backyard. *Who dug those and why?*

She walked to the large bay window to close the curtains, when the strange lights reappeared. They were brighter this evening and didn't immediately go out. She strained to see where they were coming from, but the wind was still whipping the tree branches around.

Pulling on a pair of jeans, she grabbed a light jacket to put on over her t-shirt and shoved her feet into a pair of sandals. She'd already taken the pins from her hair, but she didn't waste time putting it back up into her usual bun. There was no time. She needed to find out where those lights were coming from.

She hurried out of the house, quickly making her way down the deserted Main Street, following the lights to – the Proctor house. She watched from the sidewalk as what appeared to be a flashlight or candle moved around in the upstairs rooms. *Someone's inside. It has to be the criminal.*

She glanced at her watch and realized it was 2:00 a.m. and Kip was more than likely already fast asleep. *Maybe I can sneak inside and just see who it is, and then Kip can arrest them tomorrow morning.*

She quickly made her way to the front door, pleased to see that it had been left slightly ajar. She stepped inside and then stopped to listen. She could hear the faint muffle of footsteps above her. She started up the stairs, then stopped again. There was an old umbrella stand near the front door. She reached for a wooden cane that was covered in dust and had been there for quite some time.

Holding it in her hands, she started to go up the stairs, but all of Kip's warnings came rushing back to her mind. Taking her phone from her pocket, she quickly sent him a text message telling him where she was. She reasoned that if he were still awake, he would come to help her. If he were already asleep, he'd get the message in the morning and see that she'd tried. Either way, it would look like she'd tried to follow his orders. If his theory about the teens was correct, he'd want to be involved in stopping their nonsense himself.

She pocketed her phone and slowly climbed the stairs. As she reached the top, she could hear harried whispers coming from the end room. "It has to be here! There's no way that man didn't keep that money!"

"Maybe he spent it all," said a harsh male voice.

These were not teens.

"Three million dollars? You heard what that old busybody told us this morning. Marshall was a recluse and almost never left the house. How do you spend three million dollars if you never go anywhere?"

"I don't know, but the police found the body. That means they're going to be all over this house and property tomorrow morning."

"That's why we have to find it tonight."

Susan realized she was definitely dealing with the criminals, and she'd started to back away when a creaking sound echoed through the house. A window at the end of the hall burst open and the wind whipped along the hallway, stirring up years of dust and making an eerie sound as it moved the window back and forth. Years of neglect had rusted the hinges, and they creaked with each minute movement.

"What is that?" There was panic in the woman's voice.

"I don't know. We need to get out of here."

Susan quickly fitted her body against the small alcove in the hallway, hoping the woman would continue her search a moment longer. She needed to see the criminals so she could identify them later.

When no one exited the room, she crept closer, keeping the cane in front of her. She reached the room where the two criminals were and stopped at the doorway. They were rifling through everything in what appeared to have once been an office area.

"Why can't I get this stupid armoire open?" the woman asked, anger evident in her harsh whisper. She yanked on the doors again, but the heavy piece of furniture didn't move. "Look in the desk again. There has to be a key hidden around here someplace."

"I told you, it was probably buried with him. Are you sure you checked all of his pockets?"

"I did. And let me tell you, searching through the pockets of a dead man was just icky."

"Oh, quit your whining. Once we find where he hid the money, we'll both be living easy for the rest of our lives," the man said. "Provided your friend can actually get us out of the country."

"Don't you worry about that. We'll get out of the country, but in order to do that, we need that cash."

A loud hissing noise captured everyone's attention, and Susan cocked her head as she tried to determine where it was coming from. It sounded suspiciously like a sound Mr. Giles might make if he were being threatened, but he was nowhere to be seen.

She heard the front door open and quickly ducked back down the hallway until she could see what new threat had entered this scenario. It was Kip.

She quickly made her way back down the stairs when suddenly a scream came from above them. "Stay here!" Kip told her, rushing up the stairs as he drew his weapon.

Before he could reach the landing, the two figures that had been rifling the room rushed past him, knocking him down the stairs in their haste to leave the building. They were out the front door before she could make a move to stop them.

"Are you all right?" She hurried to Kip's side.

"I'm fine. Who were those two people?" he asked, sitting up and rubbing his shoulder where it had connected with the hard wood.

"I don't know, but before you showed up, they were rifling what looked like an office. The woman seemed convinced there was something inside this house that would lead them to three million dollars."

"What?"

"That's what she was whispering about. She seemed to think whatever they're looking for would have been buried with him. I think that's why they stole his body. They're looking for something. Maybe a map?"

"Let me take a look around and then we'll call this in and have a patrol placed here until we get to the bottom of this."

Kip headed up the stairs with Susan right behind him. The creaking of the window had gone from scary to annoying, and

Susan quickly walked down the hallway and pulled the window shut, making sure to latch it securely.

She indicated the room the two criminals had been searching and followed Kip inside. His flashlight illuminated the devastation the two had wrought on the room-- every book off the shelves, the desk drawers emptied on the floor. Only the armoire stood untouched.

"She really wanted into that piece of furniture," Susan told him.

"Well, there's probably a key here someplace, but we're not going to find it tonight. Let's get out of here."

They turned to leave, when the strange hissing sound she'd heard earlier came again. When it was followed up by the sound of nails scratching something metal, Susan felt her heartbeat pick up and she stepped a bit closer to Kip. "What is that?" she asked, her voice dropping to a whisper again.

"I don't know. Let's get out of here." They turned to leave, and then stopped as they watched a shadow begin to form on the windows. It grew in size, but they couldn't quite tell what it was until it seemed to jump from one corner of the window to another.

As the shadow settled, Susan began to laugh. "I can't believe it."

Kip looked at the shadow and then went to window, opening it and sticking his upper body outside. He came back into the room moments later with Mr. Giles in his arms.

She took her cat. "I can't believe he managed to scare me."

"Don't tell me you actually thought this house might be haunted?"

Susan looked at him. "You were acting a little spooked there as well."

Kip laughed. "Okay, you're right. Mr. Giles, you had us both going."

They exited the house. While they waited for the patrol officer to arrive, Susan sat on the porch scratching her cat's ears. As Kip joined her, he stopped and then stooped over to look at the damp ground.

"Well, look at that. It's the same tread mark we found at the cemetery."

Susan put Mr. Giles down and joined him. "Let me see."

Kip shown his flashlight towards the ground. Susan gasped. "I know who the criminals are. Or, at least, I know what they look like." She proceeded to tell him about the tourists who had come into the bakery and the man's dirty fingernails. But it was the tread mark that had been left by the woman's shoes that had her most excited.

"Are you sure it's the same mark?" Kip asked. "The forensics team said those types of shoes are only sold at exclusive boutiques located in Los Angeles, New York, and Chicago."

"Chicago?" she asked.

"Yes. They run around five hundred for a basic pair of sneakers. I can't believe any woman would pay that much money for a pair of running shoes!"

"Some women are willing to pay a lot more than that for their shoes." She grew thoughtful as the uniformed officer arrived, and Kip gave him clear instructions concerning access to the property.

After ushering her and Mr. Giles into his car, he drove her back to the bakery, but she didn't immediately get out. A thought was forming in her mind, and only Kip could answer her questions.

"What's going through that brilliant brain of yours?" he asked.

"What's the lag between someone getting parole and the notice appearing in the court records? Is it possible that Patricia Jahnke got paroled in the last few weeks, and the information wouldn't yet be available online?"

"Sure. The feds have been known to be late to file their paperwork. What are you thinking?"

"Well, we would need to check out the facts, but there was no mention of the money from the bank robbery ever being recovered. What if Marshall knew where it was and when he realized she was going to be convicted, he divorced her and took the money? He came back here after his mother passed away because it was as good of a hiding place as any.

"Maybe he was even waiting for her prison sentence to be over, playing the recluse until he could split it with her. But he died and she was stuck in prison without access to the money or its whereabouts."

Kip started his vehicle and headed for the station. "There's one sure way to find out. Let's go see if his ex-wife is still sitting in federal prison."

CHAPTER 14

Thirty minutes later, they had their answer. Patricia Jahnke had been released on parole two months ago. Her brother, Buddy, had agreed to let her live with him. Up until a week ago, she'd been faithful about meeting with her parole officer. She'd missed her last meeting, and a warrant for her arrest had already been issued.

"So, it's possible she left Illinois and came to Missouri?" Susan theorized.

"I would say that's a distinct possibility. This is her mug shot."

Susan came around his desk and then smiled as she looked at the familiar image. "That's the woman that was in the bakery. I'm sure of it. She even told me she was from Chicago."

Kip sat back in his chair. "Any idea where they were staying?"

"No, but they haven't gotten what they came here for. She was talking about leaving the country, but they needed the money to do that. I don't think they'll leave just yet."

"Let's hope not." Kip saw her hide a yawn. "Let's get you home so you can get some sleep."

"But shouldn't we be on the lookout for her?"

"We should, and I'll make sure all of the officers know to watch out for her. Lakeside is a small town, and she won't be able to hide for long. You, on the other hand, are falling asleep on your feet."

"Well, maybe I could use just a few hours."

"Let's go then. Mind if I use your couch to grab another few winks myself?"

"Not at all."

*****

Four hours later, Susan had woken up and headed down to the bakery. She hadn't removed the closed sign from the day before, so she wasn't expecting to open up. But as she stepped into the display area, she noticed several people were milling around outside. She opened the door and offered to let them in to purchase anything that was already made at half price.

She pulled several trays out of the fridge and was amazed at how many people came wandering into her shop as word of mouth traveled around town that everything in the bakery was half-off today. She'd never done that before, but she figured it would all need to be thrown out Monday, so she might as well sell what she could.

Around eleven o'clock, the crowd had started to die down. Mr. Giles had joined her to sit in his designated spot by the door, watching people as they came out and accepting their words of praise for what a beautiful cat he was.

Susan watched him grudgingly accept their touch. Once there was a break in the action, she picked him up and offered him a can of tuna for being such a tolerant feline. He simply watched her and then proceeded to dismiss her as he turned his attention to the plate in front of him.

When she heard the bell tinkle over the door again, she stepped out to greet her newest customers and stopped cold. It was Patricia and her brother.

"Good morning," she said.

"Good morning," the woman said. "We heard you were offering everything half off today, and the muffins were so good the other day, I simply had to come back. It looks like you've been pretty well picked over though."

"Yes. Well, with the water disaster yesterday, I didn't get any baking done, so there wasn't that much to start with. Would you like coffee again?"

They both nodded, the man scowling as he had the other day, the woman giving her a grateful smile. "That would be wonderful. I never can seem to get going in the morning without a good cup of coffee." It was hard to believe that this banal female was the Bored Housewife Robber.

But she was.

Susan had been looking for an excuse to go back into the kitchen, and this was it. "I've got some fresh stuff brewing in the back. Let me go grab the pot while you all decide what looks good to eat." She gave them a big smile and then ducked through the kitchen door. She rushed up the back stairs, bumping into Kip as he was stepping out of her apartment.

"Whoa!" he said.

"You have to come with me now!"

"What's wrong?"

"Nothing. Patricia and her brother are standing in the bakery."

Kip quickly decided upon a course of action. "Keep them there for as long as you can. I'll call for back up and come in through the front door." He kissed her on the forehead and ran down the stairs, ducking out the back and talking hurriedly on his cell phone.

Susan rushed back into the kitchen and grabbed her personal pot of coffee and the tray of special flavored creamers. Pushing back into the front area, she smiled at them. "I thought you might like to try a flavored creamer this morning. I personally love the amaretto."

The woman's eyes lit up. "That sounds amazing. Buddy, what flavor sounds good to you?"

Buddy scowled. "Whatever you choose is fine with me. I'll take one of those blueberry scones."

Susan plated it for him and then handed it across the counter. "Excellent choice. Even days old, they still taste fresh. And for you… I'm sorry, I don't believe we've exchanged names. I'm Susan."

The woman smiled. "I'm Patricia. I'll take the last scone. And I believe I'll try the amaretto creamer as well."

Susan handed the pastry and two cups of coffee over the counter. "So, how much longer are you two going to be in Lakeside?"

"Just until tomorrow, I'm afraid."

"Well, I hope your time here was relaxing." Susan's mind worked furiously as she tried to keep them involved in a conversation. She fumbled with her cell phone and pushed the voice record button. Who knew what information she might be able to obtain from these folks? They saw her as a simple baker, but she knew who they really were.

"So what do you do back in Chicago, Patricia?"

"Well, I haven't done much recently. I've been sick for the last several years, and my brother and I thought it might be nice to do some traveling now that I'm feeling better."

"Oh, I love to travel. Are you headed to the coast?"

"No, dear. I do believe we're going to do some traveling outside the United States. There is so much to see out there."

Susan sighed dramatically. "I would love to see Paris. I hear it's very nice this time of year."

Patricia smiled. "I've been there, and it is. They have wonderful pastries there too. You should go. You might find some inspiration for your bakery."

Susan nodded. "I'll have to think about it." She felt relieved when Kip entered the small bakery a moment later. "Detective Fletcher. How nice to see you this morning."

"Morning, Suzie. Got a cup of coffee for me?"

"Of course. Have you met my new friends yet?"

Kip looked at the very nervous couple and shook his head. "Can't say that I have."

"This is Patricia and her brother Buddy."

"Patricia and Buddy. Nice to meet you both." He glanced towards the door to see Frank had taken up a position that would prevent anyone from leaving without moving him out of the way. "So, did you hear about the activity over at the Proctor house last night?"

"No. What happened?" Susan's voice sounded breathless even in her own ears.

"Well, it seems that whoever stole poor Marshall's body has been rifling the house. They were surprised by a second set of intruders, but they left another clue behind. Another footprint."

"Did it match the one you found at the cemetery?" she asked, playing along.

"Yes, ma'am. Exactly."

"I never did get by your office to see it. Can you describe it for me?"

"Sure. It was very distinctive. There's the outline of a heart in the heel portion."

Susan looked at Patricia. "Just like your shoes. I remember from the other day. They must be popular."

Kip turned and looked at the couple. "Not really. They're very exclusive. Aren't they, Patricia?"

Buddy tried to get up and leave, but Frank stopped him at the door. Patricia sat there, her fake smile turning into a genuine sob as Kip put his cuffs on her and read her rights. As he escorted her out of the bakery, he winked at Susan. "Come see me later."

CHAPTER 15

Susan joined Kip at the station a few hours later, wanting to give him plenty of time to process his newest arrestees and take their statements. She walked in just as Patricia was being led down to the holding cells.

"Good timing," Kip told her, escorting her back to his office.

"Did they tell you what you wanted to know?"

"They sang like canaries. It seems that Marshall had been in on the bank robbery the entire time, but he got away without being detected. Patricia's face showed up on a security camera, which is how they found her."

"Bad luck."

Kip nodded. "But they were loyal to each other. She didn't give him up to get a lighter sentence, and he agreed to hold onto the money until they could enjoy it together. They had planned for him to come here with the money and wait for her to be released. They were then going to flee to Belize and spend the rest of their lives down there."

"Belize? Why there?"

"First, they speak English. Second, it's extremely cheap to live there. Three million dollars would have set them up like royalty."

"But Marshall died before she got out of prison."

"That's correct. Another piece of bad luck. He wanted to distance himself from her so that there would never be any suspicion of his involvement. He divorced her and cut off contact, so that's why she had to track him down once she got out. She tried going through the attorney who handled his other assets, but since they were no longer legally married, the man wouldn't tell her anything."

"So she came here to find the money herself."

"Yes. Marshall was a bit of a fanatic when it came to protecting things. She's almost sure that the secret to the money would have been buried with him, but they found nothing on his person. That's why they took a metal detector to the property, and that's why they dug all of the test holes. All that stupid digging is part of what weakened the water pipes, of course. But they couldn't stop looking. She thinks he buried the money on the property and that a map is hiding somewhere in the house, since it wasn't in any of his pockets."

"But I don't understand why the coroner or undertaker would know what to bury with him. That doesn't make any sense."

"Marshall didn't have any family to come forward, so he was buried in the same clothes they found him in. He collapsed in front of the grocery delivery boy, and they would have buried him just like they found him. Including anything he might have had in his pockets, or any jewelry he might have been wearing. There was no reason to save anything."

"But she didn't find anything?"

"No. She did mention that armoire, and I've had my team looking for a key all morning, but they've found nothing yet. Eventually we'll get a court order and cut it open. But for now it's a mystery."

Susan replayed his words in her head and then smiled broadly. "What type of key are they looking for?"

"An older skeleton key is their best guess."

Susan started laughing. "I think I might be able to help you there. The morning after the grave was robbed, Mr. Giles came home with his feet dirty and a brass key in his mouth. I stuck it into the treasure jar, thinking someone would be looking for it soon. I bet he was investigating the strange goings on in the cemetery, and they inadvertently dropped the key on the ground while moving the body."

"Go get that key and meet me at the Proctor house."

Susan hurried home on her bike. She grabbed the key and Mr. Giles. "You nosy old cat. You might have brought home the key to three millions dollars. I can't even imagine what that much money looks like."

*****

An hour later she stood before the open armoire in the late Marshall Proctor's office. Stacked neatly inside were carefully wrapped bricks of hundred dollar bills-- three million dollars worth of them.

The forensics team had been called back into the room. As they carefully removed the stacks of bills and did a preliminary count, it became apparent that Marshall had never spent any of the money from the bank robbery. It was indeed a crime committed for a cheap thrill, not because they had any need for the cash.

The undertaker verified that Marshall had been wearing a leather thong around his neck with a skeleton key for a pendant at the time he died. Assuming it had only sentimental value, the undertaker had placed it back around the corpse's neck for the burial. He confirmed that six years would have been long enough for the leather thong to decay to dust.

The key must have slipped off the body when it was lifted from the casket, and Mr. Giles had been on hand to claim it.

Later that evening, Kip and Susan sat in one of the restaurants down on the docks, eating fresh fish and rehashing the events of the last few days.

Kip had called the bank that had been robbed and learned they'd earned a healthy reward from their insurance company. His share would go to the Lakeside police department, since he'd worked on the crime as part of his official duties.

But Susan's share was all hers. And he had to admit he thought she'd earned it.

"You really seem to have a knack for finding clues," Kip told her.

"Thanks. I just can't seem to let a mystery lie. Neither can Mr. Giles."

"You know, things would go a lot faster if that cat of yours could talk."

"I know," she said. "But it wouldn't be nearly as much fun."

LIKE THE BOOK? KINDLY LEAVE YOUR KIND REVIEW HERE:

Brand New Secret Wedding Planner Cozy Short Story Mystery Series by Janet Evans

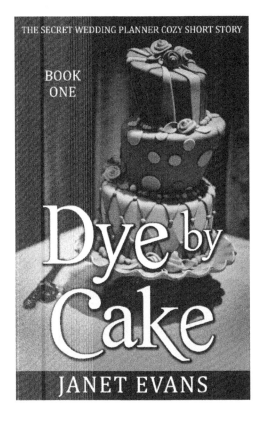

DYE BY CAKE – BOOK ONE

Groom Karl Stipple keels over moments after eating a slice of cake at his own wedding reception. Now the police have locked down the resort, and wedding planner Julia is under orders from her boss to solve the crime and clean up the mess in twenty-four hours-- or she's fired. It's a race against the clock as she finds herself entangled in a web of family mistrust, lingering old flames... and adult coloring books.

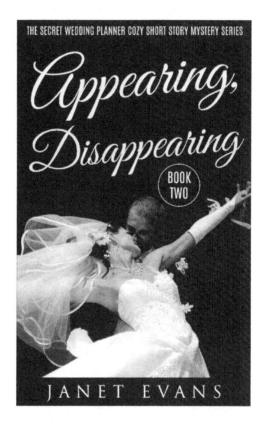

APPEARING, DISAPPEARING- BOOK TWO

For once, wedding planner Julia thinks a reception will go smoothly.
Then the bride's heirloom diamond and gold engagement ring
mysteriously vanishes. The police think they know who took it and have
closed the investigation. It's up to Julia and her friends to save an
innocent man from prison.

Brand New Secret Wedding Planner Cozy Short Story Mystery Series by Janet Evans

WEDDING SPLASH – BOOK THREE

It had been *exactly* 5 months, 4 days, and 16 weddings since the last mishap, and Julia was happy that finally, she got to plan a wedding where nothing terrible happened. This wedding is looking good. So far, no one tried to steal the bride's ring. No one tried to kill the groom.
She couldn't be more wrong. This one is the worst yet.

Made in the USA
Monee, IL
24 July 2023